I0530496

JAYTEE
Rick Edelstein
Scarlet Leaf Publishing House
2017

Copyright © 2017 Rick Ederstein
All rights reserved.

All rights reserved. No part of this book may be reproduced, stored in a retrieval system or transmitted in any form or by any means without the prior written permission of the publishers, except by a reviewer who may quote brief passages in a review to be printed in a newspaper, magazine or journal.

All characters in this book are fictitious, and any resemblance to real persons, living or dead, is coincidental.

Scarlet Leaf Publishing House has allowed this work to remain exactly as the author intended.

DEDICATION
To Rumi who does open heart Surgery on this positive nihilist.

JAYTEE

People think that a silent man is strong. Others believe he is silent because he has little to say. Jaytee fit both. Perhaps he was quiet due to his father's implant when Jaytee was nine years young. "It is better to keep your mouth shut and let people think you're stupid than to open it and prove it." Daddy was a big man and is now dead evoking no remorse from Jaytee although he inherited Daddy's body at 6' 4", 210 pounds.

Jaytee's 27th birthday was nothing more than an acknowledgement of his date of birth and recognition that in moving from Waco Texas to Los Angeles, leaving Daddy's judgments far behind was a good move. Living alone in a mid-city small apartment suited him. As he preferred defined parameters, his life was contentedly regimented. He drove a city bus five nights a week, six if the supervisor asked him to cover. Most drivers tried to avoid the late-shift but Jaytee felt comfortable with night.

He did not have to clock in until 11:45 p.m. so one very particular early afternoon Jaytee indulged in his favorite past-time, wearing his invisible cloak of solitude, walking among people and hearing smatterings of conversation. He was like a man weaving in between raindrops but these drops were non-sequitur expressions of individuals in this huge open-air Market, requiring no response or participation from Jaytee other than the pleasant indulgence of catching human moments in passing.

My soul is fatigued
Will you take a little less?
See him again? Please.

He has a psychic limp.

The air was warming, a blue cloudless sky which Jaytee found pleasantly boring as he passed a young woman strumming guitar, singing in a plaintive tone with a sign next to an open empty cigar box: "working my way through college." Jaytee didn't care for her singing but appreciated her sign, and although he wondered if it was true, he still dropped a dollar in the box and continued zigzagging with no goal in mind, just to experience the afternoon's people-watching-hearing.

Transcendental? Sooner or later we run out of stuff to transcend.

What is it with proactive as if active is not enough.

Even though I said it's no big deal between me and you the lack of pleasure is distracting.

Jaytee stopped near a stand with many cameras, film, digital, video, and one hardly recognizable, but what drew him to stop wasn't so much the cameras as the man who was selling them. He was of Mid-Eastern heritage, a wrinkled brown face with aged scars as signs of ineffable challenges and a subtle charisma. He was old but his specific age was indeterminable. His name, which Jaytee was to learn later, was Nakhur.

Two young men looking like they played college football per their team jackets with the name stitched in front stopped in front of the kiosk. The tall blond guy, stitched-Brad, was checking out the goods. His bearing was of an aggressive dude who was probably a defensive back who loved hurting the opposing half-back. He picked up the Digital Camcorder.

"Looks almost new," Brad said as if demanding a suitable response from the darker-skinned man behind the counter. Nakhur said nothing. Brad looked at his buddy, winked as if they were on a nefarious assignment. His tone was condescending, obviously a superior show off to his team-mate, "How much is this piece of goods and it looks like it may not even be working all that swift," he asked with a cynical mini-smile which, if you looked carefully, it was 'mini' as one tooth in front and one on the right visible side, both missing, made his smile appropriate for a losing clown in a circus that lost its way.

Nakhur looked at Brad curiously for a few seconds, which made Brad feel challenged as he stared back aggressively. Nakhur asked in an accented neutral voice, "What do you want?"

Brad retreated into his cultural ignorance assuming Nakhur's Mid-Eastern heritage had issues with the American language so he said loudly, as if talking to a near deaf person, and enunciated slowly assuming this brown-skinned man was not as smart as blonde Caucasian Brad, "I want to know how much this camera costs!" Brad did end with an exclamation point which, if you understood his tone, was tinged with tacit arrogant disdain.

Nakhur busied himself moving objects that required no movement and muttered, "Not for sale."

"Then why the fuck do you have it sitting there!" Brad shoved the camera back on the shelf as he and his co-conspirator walked away not caring if Nakhur heard (or perhaps wanting him to hear), "You ever feel like separating an Arab from his head." His buddy gave him five as they broke up laughing in congratulatory racism.

Jaytee observed this scene, not caring for the insulting remark. He looked at Nakhur knowing he, too, heard it. Jaytee gestured an almost apology for these punks. Nakhur got it and they had a silent connect.

An obese woman using her hands to wipe perspiration from her brow, wearing a huge florid print dress that was more like a tent, stepped in front of Jaytee who was about to pick up a camera. He stepped back giving her room. Considering her size she was very agile as she moved horizontally checking the merchandise. She picked up the same camera and asked in a very sweet, considerate tone, as if Nakhur was a long-lost friend. "This is beautiful. Almost an art object. How much are you asking, please?" She started to wipe her brow with her hands again when Nakhur reached below and extracted two tissues, offering them. She smiled coyly, took the tissues and wiped the perspiration away, giggled apologetically, "Weather is so hot nowadays don't you think I mean much hotter than last year at this time but tell your congressman about climate change and he acts like you're an alien from outer space." She wiped her perspiration with the tissues, "Thank you for these. This camera is very interesting. How much are you asking, if you wouldn't mine telling me?"

Nakhur asked, "What do you want?"

"Excuse me?" She asked.

"Out of life?" Nakhur continued.

She laughed, actually more like a flirtatious giggle. Still holding the tissues she moved them in front of her mouth and mumbled, "Is this some kind of sneaky reality show?" she asked looking around for the recording camera.

Nakhur, in a kind, considerate tone just said, "Life is a sneaky reality show. What do you want out of life?"

She laughed, "I don't know about life but this woman could use an ice cold glass of tea with a side order of blue-berry cheese cake. Have a good day," she tittered as she waddled away.

Jaytee appreciated the entire incident and became aware that Nakhur was observing him. Usually when someone approaches what Jaytee considers his personal space, he will quietly excuse himself and retreat into his comfort zones of sheltered privacy. But with Nakhur, in this moment, it was as if their bond was a settled matter and everything around them, the market, the people, the sounds, the singing, faded, all leaving Jaytee and Nakhur in an implicit bubble of discretion.

Jaytee, as if on cue, moved closer and picked up the camera. "Does it work?" he asked.

Nakhur's eyes were smiling. "For some."

"For me?" Jaytee asked, hearing his words the same time as Nakhur, not aware why he said that.

"What do you want? From life?" Nakhur asked.

"What do I want from life, wow, never thought of, well, I guess I got what I want from life pretty much although to tell you true, I would not mind being surprised every now and then." Jaytee said.

"What work do you do?"

"I drive a bus. At night."

"Why at night?" Nakhur asked.

"Night fits me."

"And the people who ride your bus at night?"

"No fuss, no bother, just pay the fare, sit down, read a magazine, get on get off, at night most everybody is polite, minding their own business, it's like a secretive world moving through scenery."

"You want to buy the camera?" Nakhur asked.

"I'm interested, yes," Jaytee responded.

"Try it out first," Nakhur said simply but there was an undefined subtext with his suggestion.

Jaytee held up the camera for better inspection, acknowledging the standard "play," "record," "rewind." He also noticed a surprising diminutive lever with a tiny arrow presently aimed at N, and, depending on movement of the lever's arrow, it can also be pointed to F or B. Not quite understanding the purpose but Jaytee was always good with his hands, comfortable that he could figure it out in practice, he held the camera to his eye and scanned the scene in the huge open-air market.

He could see through the view-finder the many people, walking, talking, bartering at stands, adults, children of all ages and ethnicity, baby strollers, a man in a wheelchair expertly wheeling in and around the throngs in motion faster than some of the strollers. Jaytee put the camera to the side and to Nakhur, "Clear and clean vision. Good camera."

Nakhur gently suggested, "Try recording. Sound automatic."

Jaytee nodded, put the camera to his eye, panned the crowds and then stopped to focus on a young, attractive Woman whose hair was gelled upwards and a look of hurt in her eyes. She was standing at a kiosk of miniscule sculptures, including intricate origami, more elegant and exquisite artistry in comparison to so many of the standard garish items in flea-markets. He heard Nakhur, "Push the lever to F."

Jaytee pushed the tiny lever arrow to F. "What does F stand for?"

Nakhur said, "And Record button."

As Nakhur didn't clarify Jaytee assumed he'll discover the purpose of F in the doing. Pushing F and Record, Jaytee squinted through the view-finder, seeing and hearing:

WOMAN talking to ASIAN MAN at his Kiosk: "These are very beautiful, delicate."

ASIAN MAN: "Yes. Want to buy?"

A MAN came weaving in the background into the shot close to WOMAN.

MAN: "Hey, funny running into you here."

WOMAN: "Not so funny. I called and you never answered."

MAN: "Guess not".

WOMAN: "We spend the night and you never even..."

MAN: "This is hardly the place to air dirty laundry."

WOMAN: "I don't hear from you the next day or at all! What kind of man are you?"

MAN: "Lighten up, we just had a good night but hey a one time shot does not an item-make."

WOMAN: "You bastard."

She slapped him.

MAN: "Bitch."

He slapped her back. She fell into the kiosk, knocking everything over and destroying many of the delicate items as the Man quickly walked away from the Woman splayed out on broken pieces. People around were reacting to this scene of mayhem.

Jaytee lowered the camera and started running over to the woman to help when, in that moment, with the camera dangling from his hand, he saw not what the camera revealed but the Woman standing at the Kiosk, everything in order and normal.

Jaytee skidded to a stop before he bumped into the woman who was aware of how close he was and said, "You're a little close for this lady's comfort, so please..."

Jaytee looked at her, around the market, crowds, adults, children everyone was participating easily, no mayhem, no Man, no harm, all the items including the delicate origami neatly on the shelf. In utter confusion he backed away in embarrassment, turned in bewilderment, stumbled back to Nakhur and held up the camera, mumbling, "What...how did...she, that woman slapped the dude, the man slapped her back and...and...she fell, broke half of everything in that stand...what the hell!"

Nakhur was content. "Do you want the camera?"

"Want the camera! I mean what I saw when I pushed the buttons you told me..." as he tried to find some reason unsuccessfully. "Something about this don't tote all that level."

"Do you want the camera?" Nakhur repeated quietly.

Jaytee looked around, at the Woman still standing by the Kiosk. At crowds of parents and children, the distant wheel chair manipulating through the throngs, back at Nakhur. "None of this computes so this country boy is just gonna' take his hat in hand be gone." He put down the camera and walked slowly away, struggling between consternation and anxiety because he saw what he saw, when suddenly, in the present moment, he heard the Woman, "You bastard."

Jaytee spun around to see the Woman slap the Man and the Man slap her back, "Bitch." She fell into the kiosk, knocking everything over and destroying much of the delicate items, as the Man walked away quickly.

Jaytee was stunned as he viewed people responding, helping the Woman up. The Man passed a dumbfounded Jaytee who looked around mid-chaos, stopping at Nakhur who was holding up the camera for him. All of this maim of....of what...Jaytee was near panic feeling he was losing touch with reality as he spun around, walking away quickly, bumping into people, obsessed with getting away from this scene which was defying his sanity.

Exiting the open-air market, Jaytee started to jog, then trot, then increasing his gait until he broke out into a full speed run, trying to grasp, to get some sense of what happened but despite his physical efforts to flee the disorder in his mind, flashes of the Woman at the Kiosk, the camera viewfinder revealing the Woman quietly at the Kiosk, then being knocked down, the Woman standing, the Man slapping her...it was a cubic hologram beyond Jaytee's ability to...Jaytee ran and ran, emotionally freaked out, through stop signs, red lights, in and out of traffic, almost knocking people over, running, running it off until a soccer ball hit him. He stopped in wild exhaustion. He looked at the soccer ball as if it was from outer space. He leaned down and picked it up trying to figure out the purpose of this round object when a young boy called out to him, "Perdon. Mi pelota."

Jaytee looked at the boy trying to fit into his reality, but with difficulty, holding the ball as a strange entity.

"Por favor," the boy called, "Senor, disculpe, mi pelota."

He ultimately realized he was holding a soccer ball, tossed it to the kid who ran back to his game leaving Jaytee standing there, bereft of understanding what occurred at the market.

Night, a blanket of security as Jaytee was driving the city bus by rote. He was still distracted by the Market experience, almost comforted by the non-sequitur conversations from his passengers:

You got to believe to receive.

God ain't dead.

Maybe he's just sleeping late.

He made love with his socks on.

Ni un paso atras.

Jaytee usually had no issues sleeping at the end of his shift after he closed the shades to the early morning light and crawled into bed tired, exhausted but not from work. His mind wouldn't sleep as he tossed, turned and even moaned in the madness of a nightmare, flashes of present, future, past revelations through the camera. He had other dreams which awakened him in severe disturbance.

Jaytee had no choice but to return to the open-air Market. He cautiously merged with the people through the aisles of many kiosks knowing where he was, reluctantly weaving in and out of the crowds with obvious destination, hearing but paying no mind to people's words:

He was a coward.

People hurt you when you're brave.

He wasn't brave, he was dumb.

You can't unwring a bell.

Twenty feet away Jaytee stopped, trying to get some kind of emotional balance which he clearly did not experience. He attempted to breathe easily but the effort was countermanded by his sense of unease and urgency. He inched closer, now about ten feet where he could clearly see Nakhur and hear customers at his kiosk including a man who said, "I'd like to check out that camera."

Nakhur glanced up beyond the man to where Jaytee was standing. They locked eyes as Nakhur said without looking at the potential customer but into Jaytee's eyes, "It is already sold." To which the man said, "Should put a red tag on it or something," he walked away. Nakhur continued to link eyes with Jaytee who cautiously moved close enough for him to be heard.

Jaytee hissed with a quietly insistence, "Talk to me!"

Nakhur gently said, "I will, my friend, but what I have to tell you is not for this open air market. Are you driving your bus this evening?"

"No, I'm off for two days," Jaytee said.

"Good." Nakhur wrote an address on a piece of paper, handing it to Jaytee. "Come and have Turkish coffee with me. At eight eleven."

Jaytee arrived a few minutes early but decided, since Nakhur specifically said eight eleven. He waited until his watch hit it and then knocked on the door. He heard a muffled voice mixed in with music foreign to his ears. "The door is open." Jaytee cautiously entered seeing Nakhur preparing coffee. "Sit, my friend, at the table." Nakhur said. Jaytee looked around at Nakhur's loft, an eclectic strange and yet intriguing setting with pieces from many different cultures adorning the walls, lamp shades making a statement on their own, original string instruments leaning against the walls, gentle almost-hypnotic music playing from a stereo on which a stringed drape from Morocco languished.

Jaytee approached the very low table ready to sit, but no chairs were available, just huge floor pillows. Jaytee was hesitant. Again hearing Nakhur, "Yes, find your way." Jaytee hesitantly sat on the pillow, struggling to find the best way to arrange his long legs, straight ahead was unwieldy. Jaytee was not a floor-sitter but finally, to Nakhur's observant humor, sat cross-legged with his elbow awkwardly on the table.

Nakhur, wearing a flowing caftan of colors worth a canvas in a gallery, came to the table with two small steaming ups of Turkish coffee, setting them down, sitting opposite of Jaytee, on a pillow as he gracefully crossed his legs. They were silent although within Jaytee, silence left home with the camera's phantasmagorical experience. Nakhur stirred the coffee, stopped, sipped, emitted a pleasing sound and then gestured to try the coffee.

Jaytee who erupted, "The camera!"

"Names first."

Jaytee blurted, "Jay Thomas Bergstrom. Everybody calls me Jaytee."

"Good. Nakhur."

"Nak-what?" Jaytee asked.

"My name. Nakhur. A Persian name."

"Does it mean something, Mister Nakhur?"

"Not mister. Just Nakhur, a camel that won't give milk until her nostrils have been tickled," Nakhur said.

He drank from the very small cup, two sips and it was empty. "The camera," Jaytee persisted.

"Yes, the camera," Nakhur indicated the object on a shelf in the corner of the room.

"The camera," Jaytee struggled, "...it shot, recorded a scene that...that did not happen."

"And then?" Nakhur prodded.

Jaytee threw up his hands in mock surrender. "It happened."

Nakhur looked at Jaytee questioningly. Decided. Stood, walked to a home-made altar wreathed with unfamiliar small carvings, intricate interwoven slats of swirling wood and bamboo pushing energy upwards. He lit a candle, mumbled something unintelligible to Jaytee, listened, acquiesced, returned to the table where Jaytee was observing in guarded curiosity.

Nakhur picked up Jaytee's small cup with residue of the Turkish coffee at the bottom and stared into it, moved it around, gazed with intense focus as he 'read' the grounds. "Ah," he exhaled, "Yes, you are the true person." He moved the cup observing the ambiguous grounds. "But the end is..." he looked intensely at Jaytee, "You know more than you know..." again he moved the cup slightly shifting the sediments, looked deeply into it and back to Jaytee. "But not enough!"

Jaytee felt as if he was inundated by a deluge of molasses long past their expiration date. He awkwardly unfolded his lengthy legs, stood with effort, not knowing where to go, what to do with his hands except a movement of emotional frustration bordering on losing touch with any frame of reference that was recognizable. "Look, Nakhur, I am trying with every ounce of limited intelligence I may have to make sense of something that just don't make sense. I may not know scat from scout but what happened with that camera is..." He tried to decelerate his breathing, "...what happened...trying to understand something that has no understanding in its hip pocket is like trying to get a river to run over bridge during dry season if you get my drift." Jaytee exploded, "For God's sakes man, that bloody camera predicted the future or has mamma's boy lost his marbles!"

Nakhur looked at him with approving empathy. "Do you like the ocean?"

"Do I like the ocean? That's like asking a condemned man if he likes the twine count on a noose." Jaytee snapped.

"Tomorrow we shall be on the boardwalk on Venice Beach."

"Mister...Nakhur, lookahere, I am not trying to be more than what I am but you are making me feel less. So pleasure sir, Nakhur, help out this imitation of a sane man and tell me..."

"Eleven nineteen a.m. Meet me in front of the parking facility."

"Unless you give me a better reason than liking the ocean, Nakhur, this down home boy needs not to..."

Nakhur softly interrupted him, "You will come to a greater Understanding. Tomorrow. I promise."

"I don't know whether you're having me on or just..." Jaytee threw up his hands in frustrated dismay and just grunted.

"When Nakhur makes a promise, it is done." he said ending their evening.

Nakhur was in a different pastel colored caftan and New Balance sneakers, holding the camcorder. He dipped his head slightly to the approaching Jaytee who was wearing faded jeans, a T-shirt, and old Jordans. "You are a man who respects time," Nakhur said as it was, indeed, eleven nineteen.

"My Daddy claimed that being late is a disrespect to the other so you be on time even if it hair lips every mule in Texas. I see you got the camera."

"We will walk," Nakhur led the way through a jumble of tourists, lost characters wrapped in blankets, tattooed skaters, a dog with sunglasses riding on a skateboard pulled by a man jogging in a curved line, young women in bikinis a bit thicker than dental floss, strumming guitars and aggressive singing, as snippets of conversation from passing people crisscrossed through the air:

He listens but he doesn't hear.

You want me to buy you a book.

I already got one.

"All right, Nakhur, you made a promise. I may be as green as a cut-seed watermelon but I ain't goin' back on my raisin' which means when a man makes a promise his word is like his next breath so as much as I like the ocean you promised a greater understanding."

As they weaved through the ocean-lovers, the observers, the barely clinging to life, the ultimate drop-outs, Nakhur spoke in a smooth tenor. "You understand the meaning of mystical?"

Jaytee stepping over dog poop, "Something that isn't really real, I guess."

"It is real," Nakhur emphasized, "Just not apparent to the conditioned senses..." he avoided a skater swishing by, "It has a connection to the ultimate source."

Jaytee observing a stand holding hundreds of miniature garishly painted skulls. "Who buys these things? Ultimate source. What is that?"

Nakhur sat on a bench, "To give it a name is blasphemy."

Jaytee sat next to him. "If this is your version of greater understanding this son of a dust 'n mud daddy can't come it. Nakhur, clarity is the call of the day so if you..."

He was interrupted by a beautiful, young, barely-clad bikini'd lady on roller-blades who came to a screeching halt in front of them. She held out her hands unsteadily. Her voice was in imperfect wavering harmony. "Can either of you splendid gentlemens help a lady out?"

Nakhur asked in an almost naïve voice, "For what purpose?"

She laughed louder than her lack of humor. "For the purpose of making yours truly feel good, this girl is talking real good if you can hear my tune."

Nakhur offered her a ten. "If my friend can take some pictures of you with his camera." Adjusting the arrow to F he gave Jaytee the camcorder.

Her lack of control loud voice was demanding rather than inviting. "Hey, man, increase the crease and he can do more than take my picture if you get my slant and this girl ain't talking metaphorically!"

"Just your picture," he said, holding up the ten and indicating to Jaytee to start operating the camera. "Record, Jaytee."

She took the ten as Jaytee, with Nakhur nodding, saw the arrow on F, pushed the Record button, looked through the viewfinder to see:

Lady Skater rolls away to a near-by cemented, granite rotunda, with a raggedly group of users and dealers hanging on, sitting, standing, leaning on the granite formations.

Skater gives one man the ten for a drug exchange.

Skater sits on granite bench, ingests drugs, as others ignore her.

Skater passes out on the bench, drooling .

Jaytee lowers the camera. Looks up. Lady Skater is still in front of him. Jaytee looks at Nakhur whose eyes reflect affirmation, then looked at the Lady Skater.

"Hey, man, increase the crease and he can do more than take my picture if you get my slant and this girl ain't talking metaphorically, blues!"

"Just your picture."

She takes the ten, affects a mock pose, "Thanks for the bank. I'm outta' sight in more ways than one," and rapidly skates away toward the rotunda.

Jaytee trying to ignore his anxiety, gave Nakhur the camera and very slowly and apprehensively walked toward the rotunda to see the users, dealers and the Lady Skater passed out drooling. One of the dealers notices Jaytee. "You in the market, bro?"

Jaytee stares at the stoned Lady on the granite, shakes his head and having difficulty locating his next breath, walks away from them.

Nakhur joins him as they walk through the throngs, Jaytee finally exclaiming in his muddled threat to reason, "Why me? I don't, I won't, it doesn't compute on any level that is part of this man's A B C's... I...I feel like I'm a blind man playing a full stakes hand with a seeing eye dog...talk to me, dawg, why me, Nakhur?"

"Why not?" Nakhur replied.

Jaytee was silent a few beats, then echoed, "Why not, he says." They continued walking, as if a bubble of solitude embraced them, silently treading through a peopled boardwalk. Jaytee stopped. "Why not." He said not as a question but rather a conclusion. Jaytee ultimately coming to terms with something that fits no paradigm of plausible reality. "Okay, all right, why not me...so me is here, not understanding but I can't be arguing with a reality exceeding reality if I'm making any sense which ain't all that possible in this chasm of confusion."

"Good," Nakhur said simply.

"Good, he says. Whew, I don't know if good is good but since't I ante'd up I got to play out the hand," Jaytee said trying to find a rational balance with limited success. "All right, yes said me agreeing to the unread small print...the time to kill a snake is when he raises his head so let it roll," Jaytee sighed in reluctant resignation. "Okay Nakhur, what's next?"

"When?" Nakhur asked.

"When? How about now?" Jaytee said with petulance in the face of handling something without a book of instructions.

Nakhur looked ahead towards the pier, smiled easily, "I like those little rides."

Nakhur and Jaytee were sitting next to each other as the small geared wheel gently moved them up and around. It was a smooth excursion with no bumps, just an easy flow above and around the arc. Jaytee took a deep breath, indicating the camera in Nakhur's lap, "This is like a log so crooked it won't lay still I mean, I may as well say it, this here camera time-travels, just saying it makes me feel like I'm trying to scratch my ear with my elbow."

"Want to discontinue, leave, depart as if we never met, forget about this entire experience?" Nakhur asked.

Jaytee smirked, "Forget about...a person cannot forget something that has already taken deep roots in the soil of his experience."

"Then what is your choice, Jaytee?" Nakhur asked.

As he was effortlessly being moved on this small ride he said,

"Or as my peoples say, are you gonna fish or cut bait. Uhmm hmmm," Jaytee murmured, " Sometimes a man makes a choice and some other times the choice makes the man. It's a done thing, Nakhur. This good 'ole boy's along for the ride waving goodbye to the questions that bump in the night."

Nakhur nodded as a seal to their implicit agreement and held up the camera for Jaytee indicating the levers and arrows. "F is Forward is Future. N is now is Present. B is before is Past."

"B is past you say. Before? Meaning what exactly?"

Nakhur said, "The significant before now...will present itself."

"I'm not sure what that means," Jaytee said.

"Trust."

"Trust?" Jaytee questioned.

"The past that is never really past will be revealed."

"You want me to buy into that because I just don't feel all that in sync with what you're putting down," Jaytee pushed.

Nakhur did not raise his voice but his assertive tone was enough. "Enough with word levels. Experience, Jaytee, you will know," handing the camera over to Jaytee with solemnity.

Jaytee got it to some degree. "Okay, okay I switch to B and the camera shows me a person's before-now-past of their life that is significant, right?"

"Yes, and be aware that you cannot change a moment of the past but, and listen good my friend...are you listening?" Nakhur prompted.

"I plow a deep row on the listening side," Jaytee assured him.

Nakhur's timbre resonated, "Although you cannot change a moment of the past, it may help you decide if you want to change a person's future."

Jaytee stopped, ran Nakhur's words through his mind scrambling for reason which denied logic. He stared at Nakhur, then at the camera, back to Nakhur, slowly asking with trepidation. "You telling me I can change a person's future?"

"Two times, yes, you can interfere, two times."

"Why only two?"

"That is all that is given," Nakhur said as the ride ended and they both got off continuing their walk through the tourists, bikers, peddlers of tacky goods, hearing bits and pieces:

He was born on the day God had a hangover.

Seven almonds a day.

Carried too far stupid is lethal.

"This is heavy," Jaytee said "but daddy didn't raise no sissy so I figure I can carry the weight. Hang in with me, Nakhur, I'm just settling things in for the long count. B is past, F is future, two times I can change the future, right?" Nakhur nodded. "Okay, okay, I got it," Jaytee said, "I am all in."

"Good," Nakhur commented as they walked hearing words of people on the boardwalk.

He dresses like a ventriloquist's dummy.

Some days I feel like I'm drowning on dry land.

The butt crack is the new cleavage.

In the middle of his thought Jaytee blurted "But suppose, just suppose, I'm not sure what I'm getting at but hang in with me, Nakhur, I mean ever since I was a kid I used to bring home wounded creatures, a bird fell out of a nest or even one time a hunter killed a mama wolf and left the pup to die. I took that little thing and fed it with a bottle and nipple or in high school even another kid in my class was not too swift, maybe damaged I think and some guy was making fun of him steady which was just not right so I straightened out that dude to lay off. I mean that's what a person does, it's only human nature, right?"

"Some humans, Jaytee. What are you trying to say?" Nakhur asked.

"Well," Jaytee took a breath and went for it, "Suppose, just supposin' a little innocent baby is in harm's way, I mean a drunk driver about to crash into his carriage and I used up the two times."

"You are not permitted a third," Nakhur said firmly.

Jaytee persisted, "But just suppose, I am not a man who takes harm to babies easily, s'posin' I go for the not-permitted third and the baby lives. C can I get an amen!"

Nakhur stopped, looked hard at Jaytee, his energy was powerful, shutting out other sounds and sights on this busy boardwalk, speaking with lasered intent, "You will no longer be protected."

"What does that mean?" Jaytee asked.

"You do not want to find out."

They continued their walk when Jaytee stopped, looking at the many tables of the outdoor café occupied by couples and a few by single men and women. He looked at Nakhur who understood without verbalization, nodded once. Jaytee lifted the camera, aimed it at a very attractive South American woman. He checked the lever's arrow currently pointed at N. He pushed the Record button, looking through the viewfinder, sound automatic.

WOMAN sitting at table when MAN approaches. "Looks like you can stand some company."

WOMAN looks at him and just turns away.

MAN sits, "You're alone, I'm alone, let's be alone together."

WOMAN looks at him disdainfully.

MAN says, "We can make a lot of small talk but we both know what we want. Let's cut to the chase. Hotel room's ten minute walk from here."

WOMAN smiles and talks softly in Spanish. "Aun si tu pico fuera tan grande como tu ego no serias ni la mitad de un hombre." [If your dick was as big as your ego you still would not be half a man.]

MAN says, "I don't understand Spanish, that is Spanish right? But the way you say it makes me hard. One more time, baby."

WOMAN says in obvious disgust, "Guevon," [Birdbrain] rises and walks away.

MAN says to her departing rejection, "Probably gay."

Jaytee stops shooting, looks at Nakhur who nods. Jaytee adjusts his camcorder from N to F for future, pushes Record, through the viewfinder he pans the camera to a different table with another single attractive woman drinking ice coffee, he pans back to the offending "probably gay" Man.

Same MAN looks around, sees another attractive woman at a different table, he walks over. "Looks like you can stand some company."

"I don't think so," she says.

MAN sits down, "Hey, you're alone, I'm alone, let's be not alone together."

WOMAN: "Listen, Mister, you better split before..."

MAN: "Come on baby, let's cut to the chase and save the small talk. We're..."

A BRUISER of a dude walks into the frame. "What's this punk doing here?"

WOMAN: "He's just some uninvited asshole who..."

BRUISER grabs MAN, pulls him up despite his resistance, punches him hard knocking him down into a nearby table as a pitcher of beer tilts over and soaks the downed Man who is bleeding from the nose and mouth.

BRUISER: "Punk!" as he and the WOMAN leave.

Jaytee moves the camcorder from his eye. Puts the lever-arrow to N and glances at the table in the present time-frame revealing the former woman walking away, "Guevon." And the Man seated, "Probably gay."

Jaytee looks at Nakhur who nods affirmative for unspoken permission. Jaytee holds the camera, pushes arrow to B, to reveal the past as he focuses on the Man sitting at table who is scoping out potential women for sex. Jaytee Records, with his eyes glued to the viewfinder sees:

Summer night kitchen with a tired, attractive woman cleaning up after a solitary dinner; A knock on the screen door, she opens it to the backyard revealing the MAN. "What do you want?" she asks giving him no room to enter.

"Can I come in?" he asks.

"Your re-entry subscription has run out."

"Come on, I just want to talk to you."

She is not giving, "About missing six child-support payments?"

"Let me in, baby, and we can discuss things like adults instead of..."

She keeps the screen door locked, "I am talked out, cried out, tired out of telling your son it's not his fault that Daddy left not once but twice."

"If you'll just give me one more chance I know we can..."

"The return window is closed," she slammed the heavy door, locked it, and walked away.

Jaytee pulls the camera away from his face, moving lever arrow to N. He looks over to the café and sees the Woman walking away, "Guevon," as the Man mutters, "Probably gay." Jaytee shakes his head and starts to walk away with Nakhur following when a ruckus of confronting commotion is heard. He turns to see: The Bruiser punching and knocking the Man down as a pitcher of beer spills on his bleeding nose and mouth, "Punk" the Bruiser hurls as he leaves with this Woman.

Jaytee and Nakhur turn away and walk along the Boardwalk ignoring conversations of people passing:

I'm totally broke.

With her kinda' body she could have...

If you can't handle the heat get outta' the kitchen.

They continued their walk when Jaytee, troubled, searching for a linear explanation within a cylindrical force. He ultimately asked, "How will I know who to do?"

"You will know," Nakhur said with emphasis.

"Suppose checking out the past will influence me to change the future or deal with the now and I'm not sure what I'm saying but maybe I mean, if I sound confused it's because I am, okay, here's my concern, Nakhur...can it be against the law changing somebody's life before it happens?" Jaytee asked.

"Which law?"

Jaytee tumbled out his concerns. "Okay, not a regular crime on the books, no, but let's say the Bible, my Momma made me read with her and I got to remembering more than I want like Ecclesiastes, for everything there is a season and a time for every matter under heaven. I mean will I be breaking the, well you know, changing a season for a particular person may be breaking the Bible's law, do you think?".

Nakhur said, "Pikkuah Nefesh."

"Pikkuah what?"

Nakhur responded, "A great Rabbi said, to save a life you can violate almost any commandment."

Jaytee's precious night easily enveloped him as he drove the city bus. On the floor next to him was the camera. Stopping for riders to leave and other to board, Jaytee was on automatic as people deposited fares, some cards to be read, acknowledged amid sounds of exterior traffic. Inside the bus snatches of conversation, some from passengers to each other, some on cellphones.

It's just chaos but with better sound.

It's do it or not, that simple.

I'd divorce her but I can't afford it.

Jaytee stopped the bus at the designated sign, admitting a passenger, a very attractive Woman who from her carriage and dress has seen better times but can't remember when, carrying an old suitcase and a shopping bag stuffed with clothes. She put many coins in the slot.

Jaytee observed, "Need another twenty-five cents."

The Woman spoke with an East European accent, "I...I have no more twenty five cents change."

Jaytee looked at her, knowing it's not a scam, reached in his pocket and dropped his own quarter into the slot. "That'll cover it."

The Woman nodded and sat as Jaytee drives on, checking her in the rear view mirror.

After many stops, passengers getting on and off, Yanna remains seated in the back as bits of conversation course inside the bus.

I broke up laughing and she was pissed.

His smile would make a crocodile blush.

I just feel out of tune as if I lost harmony with the world.

Hours later, at the end of his shift with daylight breaking through, Jaytee drove the bus to the designated parking place in the Depot. He is aware that the Woman sitting in the back hugging her shopping bag with her feet on the scarred suitcase is the only passenger remaining. "Last stop, Miss."

"Do you not turn around and go back?" she asked hesitantly.

"No, ma'am, end of my shift. Checking out time for this good 'ole boy, thank you."

She nods, gathers her suitcase, shopping bag and gets off as Jaytee watches her walk to a distant bench at the return direction bus stop. Jaytee took his checkout material, the camera and got off.

Thirty minutes later Jaytee exited the Terminal locker room, having changed from his driver's uniform, carrying the camera, walked to the bus stop and sat next to the Woman on the bench in front of a bus that just pulled over. The door opens and the Driver got off making entries into a paper on his clip-board. "Hey, Jaytee, wassup?"

"Nothing much, C-V."

"Taking off in ten. Forgot my coffee. Watch the store," going into the Terminal office, Jaytee got on the bus and sat next to the window looking at Woman sitting on the bench. Thinking about it and giving into to his impulse he picked up the camera, moved the lever to B – past, aimed it at the seated Woman, pushed Record button and through the viewfinder Jaytee saw:

Pregnant Yanna walking out of a small restaurant, arm in arm with her husband, down the street, turning the corner into a shaded walkway when they are confronted by two thugs demanding money.

Her husband pushes one away as the other grabs her purse and tears off her necklace.

Her husband and Thug wrestling on the ground.

The thug near Yanna pulls a gun aiming it at her husband.

Yanna screaming leaps on his back, tearing his hair, his face but he still pulls the trigger instantly killing her husband.

Thug feels the pain from clawing Yanna, drops the gun as he hurls Yanna off his back.

Yanna falls to the ground, sees and picks up the gun as the Thug comes towards her. Yanna screams as she aims the gun, pulls the trigger hitting the rushing Thug square in the chest as he falls dead.

The other thugs who was under her now-dead husband extracts himself as he sees wild Yanna with a gun pointed at him and runs away despite Yanna screaming and shooting at his departing figure.

She drops the gun, kneels and rocks her dead husband, sobbing.

She feels a sharp stabbing pain and grasps her pregnant stomach, doubling over in acute pain.

"Got yourself a toy, do you." Returning driver remarks, as Jaytee bolted out of Yanna's past trauma and puts down the camera as the Driver with a thermos of coffee gets on the bus and starts the engine warming it up. Before he pulls out Jaytee said, "Hold up, C-V."

"What's up? I'm about to go on my run."

Jaytee walking to the door, "Give me a minute."

"Just a minute. I go over time and Mister Asshole in there gives me what for."

Jaytee walked over to the Woman at the bench, pointing to the bus. "I uhmmm, I think maybe you might need a ride."

She looks at him, sighs, "Yes. No. I have no money."

"Where do you want to go?" He asked.

The Woman exclaimed in the middle of her grief, "She did not pay her what do you call it, the morg something...for the house I think."

"Mortgage?"

"We pay rent but Bank Man with papers and Police say we must leave. One old man living in room next to me for a long time he throws himself off bridge."

"Tough times," Jaytee uttered.

"Tough times yes," the Woman mumbled with a tired cynicism.

The horn of the bus sounded with the Driver calling, "Minute's about up, Jaytee."

"Comin, C-V," and to the Woman, "Look, this may sound out of line but...I mean I don't mean nothing wrong, just...well...I have a bed and a couch. You could have the bed. For the night. That's all. Nothing more intended."

She looked at him to determine if he is safe. And then shrugged as 'safe' meant nothing in the face of her profound loss. Barely anything mattered beyond her built-in instinct to survive which was in contrast to the old man who jumped off the bridge.

The bus stopped close to Jaytee's apartment building. "Your stop, Jaytee."

"Thanks C-V. Have a good run." Jaytee indicated to the seated Woman to follow him as he got off the bus carrying his camera. She hesitated as the Driver called back to her, "On or off lady, I got a schedule." She got off carrying her shopping bag and suitcase.

Jaytee awkwardly led the way as the Woman followed. Then stopped and reached out, "Here let me carry some of that stuff," but she clutched it to her body making her worn clothing a personal identity, "No!"

Jaytee nodded, "Just wanted to help. No problem." He walked ahead with her following behind him in this early morning as car traffic and pedestrians were starting on their day of work, passing two women talking:

It's just a matter of being equal, I said.

Equal! If I was equal to him I'd kill myself.

Jaytee, holding the camera, unlocked the door, swung it open and entered his apartment, holding the door for the Woman who entered. The apartment was neat, clean and sparse, a queen-sized bed, couch, a dresser, table, chairs hard and soft, heavy shades still up permitting the sun to break through, a kitchenette area with stove, small refrigerator, cabinets, just the bare necessities for the kind of single man Jaytee is. He closed the door behind her indicating, "Nothing much but it will do," as she stood frozen hugging her shopping bag and tattered suitcase. "You can sit, that there chair ain't much but it'll hold a body, or on the bed, I don't be meaning anything, or the couch, whatever."

The tension was uncomfortable. Jaytee was not equipped with social graces in this awkward situation as she sat on the edge of the chair. He was unsure what to do and indicated,

"Bathroom, closet, you can hang some stuff up and if you want, the dresser over there." He walked to it and opened some drawers. "I only use a few drawers. See, there's room."

The silence was oppressive until she too quietly asked, "Why do you do this?"

"I don't think much about what I do. I just do it."

"Just do it," she repeated suspiciously.

Jaytee did not know how to make her ... what, he thought, easier, relax, not with what he saw about her past...he walked toward the bathroom, opened the door continuing his tour-guide which was a more comfortable routine in this decidedly trying situation, "Bathroom. Clean towels. Even a new toothbrush I haven't gotten around to using yet."

"I have toothbrush," she said in a tone asserting her independence.

"Well, there you go!" The awkward silence was not abating. "Okay, uhmm, you see I drive the late night shift and about this time I grab me some forty...and so..."

"Forty?" she asked in her East European accent.

"Oh, yeah, sorry. Forty winks, just a saying."

"Meaning what to say?" she asked suspiciously.

"Get me some sleep. Six hours usually cracks it. So I'll be pulling down the shades and uhmmm...you can take the bed, the couch'll suit me just fine thank you."

She harshly asked, "What do you want from me?"

"From you?" Jaytee was surprised and put off by her accusatory tone, "I don't be wanting nothing from you, miss. Just laying out the lay of the land."

"You want nothing from me."

"Just offering some down home hospitality."

"That I should believe?" she retorted suspiciously.

Jaytee wasn't having this, "Makes me no never mind what you believe since't this boy knows what I know." He pulled down the heavy shades throwing the apartment into near darkness and arranged things on the couch for him. "I'm a working man who needs to crash his tired bones...and you look like you can stand a few z's yourself." She sat quiet on the edge of the chair. Jaytee shrugged, "Your call," and went to the bathroom closing the door behind him as she sat there, hearing running water, hearing screams of her past, totally unsure behind her protective distrust.

Shadowed hours later, she was fully clothed in the queen-sized bed trying to sleep, but to no avail. She sat up and looked over at Jaytee in his T-shirt and shorts, scrunched on the couch too small for his body with a thin blanket almost covering him, not sleeping well as he tried different positions. She sat up, looked at Jaytee who was unsuccessfully attempting to move his long legs into a curl on the couch. He turned and became aware that she was looking at him. "Come," she said.

"You sure?" Jaytee whispered.

"To sleep only."

Jaytee gratefully went to the other side of the bed and curled in. "To sleep."

"Only," she said softly.

"Only," Jaytee muttered as he nestled into the mattress' familiar indentation fitting his long body, hoping to fall into the desired slumber.

Hours later, lying back to back, both were restless. Jaytee opened his eyes as he heard Yanna moaning, sounds rather than words, as if she is fighting some oppressive force and then she screamed. Jaytee turned to her and just nudged her slightly and said consolingly, "It's okay, just a bad dream. It's okay."

She opened her eyes in a frightened glare, trying to ascertain who Jaytee is, near panic her rapid breath was audible as he quietly said, "Jaytee here. You were having a bad dream. Everything is okay now. Easy, girl, you can be safe now."

She was confused, frightened, "Safe?"

"It's okay...nothing to worry...I promise."

She looked at Jaytee...trying to control her anxiety... "I...oh god...I am sorry, I was, please, do you want me to go?"

"Go?" Jaytee assured her, "No, I just want to make things maybe a little bit, I don't know maybe a little more laid back maybe for you, so you and even this working man can get some sleep and..."

Her breathing became difficult as she tried to restrain her sudden need to scream, to cry, to...she sat up...inhaling, exhaling...sounds of hurting, agony, groans... Jaytee carefully touched her back, moving his huge hand gently, trying to soothe her when she lost control and screamed burying her face in her hands, sobbing loudly. Jaytee turned her around, put his arm over her shoulder. Sobbing Yanna looks up at him in alarm. "Shhh....shhh...I understand...shhhh..." The Woman in raw moaning agony buried her head in Jaytee's chest. He held her and gently rocked, "It's gonna' be okay, shhh, I promise...you can rest now...shhhh..."

Six hours later she awoke to see Jaytee laying out breakfast on the small table. "What..." she mumbled, "I am, I don't know but..."

"Just in time. Coffee. Black. I don't have milk, sorry."

She got her bearings, walked to the bathroom, "I drink black."

She came out minutes later, uncertain.

"Pull up a chair before it gets cold," Jaytee said.

She sat as if waiting for something to happen. Jaytee ate and indicated for her to do the same. She was in a fog of acceptance, started eating very carefully in this late afternoon. After the sounds of forks on plates and coffee cups lifted and set down, the uncomfortable silence was cracked when Jaytee broke it. "What is your name, anyhow?"

"I do not know what to do," she said.

"About what?"

"I will wash the dishes and then I should go, yes?" She said.

"Go where?" Jaytee asked.

"I do not know," she said looking down avoiding his eyes.

"Hey, what is your name, come on, and you can look at me, I ain't the big bad wolf."

"Yanna."

"Anna, good."

"No, Yanna. Yanna Ivanova."

"Okay. Jaytee," he said as if talking to himself out loud. "Uhmmm, well, I may be about to say something stupid but my momma taught me that God looks after drunks, fools and babies and guess which one I qualify for."

"I do not understand what you are saying." Yanna said.

Jaytee was doing a verbal selfie. "Okay, okay out with it, boy..." and then to her, "Listen Yanna, maybe you should think of, well, what I'm trying to say is that you can actually, you know, stay."

"Stay where?"

"Here"

"Stay here, with you?" She asked.

"Uhmm hmm. Yeah."

"Why?"

"Why...okay, why...let's see..."

"You feel pity for me?" She asked resentfully.

"No, it ain't about you, it's about me," Jaytee said.

"What is about you, please?"

Jaytee admitted an embarrassed smile as he was about to divulge something personal which was like a foreign language to him. "I uhmmm...I been living alone all this time and it's been just, well, okay good I guess, I mean no complaints, s'all okay, but then again there have minutes, moments maybe to tell you true, Yanna, not always, but sometimes in the hard light of day, what I'm saying is that too much alone can make me meaner'n a yaller yard dog." Jaytee snorted. "Dog, yeah, I thought maybe of getting a dog, you know for company but then I thought with me working out there what would the dog be doing and I'd come home to walk him to pee and poop and then I need to sleep and the dog probably been sleeping the whole time I'm out there working so the idea of a dog is more interesting than actually getting a dog and what I'm trying to say but having difficulty as you can rightfully see, Yanna, is that I would like to come home to more than just me."

Yanna said nothing. Loudly.

Jaytee felt vulnerable after the personal revelations and Yanna's lack of affirmation sat on him like an anvil of rejection. He covered with a touch of macho attitude, "Your call. This man has to go to work." Yanna remained seated. Too quiet for Jaytee's druthers as he grabbed his jacket, walked to the dresser drawer and took out a key, putting it on top. "Here's an extra key if you decide to stay." Yanna just looked at him silently. Jaytee gestured an expression of nonchalance to cover his feeling of rejection, took the camera and left.

Jaytee driving the city bus, grateful for the blanket of a cloudy night. He felt like a fool offering Yanna to stay with him in the face of what he perceived as her silent refusal. What the hell, he thought, my life is great, no problem, what did I do...it was just...if it ain't broke, don't fix it and there I went trying to fix...he shook off his inner thoughts and what was automatic now became his focus, driving through traffic, picking up passengers and instead of ignoring their comments, listened gratefully to the meaningless words distracting him from his personal embarrassment.

He had his nose broken twice.

She has selective hearing.

I don't like to cook, won't even make toast.

Jaytee drove through the night, stopping, starting, admitting passengers, departing passengers, trying to focus on it all but throughout the night flashes of Yanna sobbing in his chest; flashes of Jaytee holding her, Yanna's sleeping head resting on his shoulder.

WALKING TO HIS BUILDING in the overcast morning passing people going to work.

I forgot my mother's maiden name so I can't access my account.

Natural childbirth? Please...nothing more natural than natural pain killer, thank you.

Jaytee adjusted the camera strap so it hung over his shoulder as, with apparent trepidation, he inserted the key, opened the door, walked in. He looked and saw just his simple apartment, dishes dried and stacked neatly. No Yanna. The bathroom door was closed so he called, "Yanna, are you there?" No response. He opened the bathroom door. No Yanna. He opened the closet, the dresser drawers hoping to find her clothing. Nothing. He stood still, more than disappointed, dealing with a feeling of hurt which was not a familiar experience as Jaytee unconsciously created a life expunging daddy and carefully crafted an existence of simple reliability, paying his bills on time, never missing a day at work, all as a dependable cloak assuring the absence of hurt. But now, he felt like an ax split his head from Yanna's negation, hearing down-home criticisms, well boy you sure enough ripped yo' britches...feeling like a whupped dog...hearing his Daddy, "Sometimes you are so thick you can't see through a bob-wire fence, boy!" Jaytee slammed the door as he ran out of the apartment.

Walking in a rage, the camera still an adjunct to his body, not knowing where he was going and caring less, passing people, bumping into some, hearing others as he tried to distract, detach from Yanna's absence.

Hey if you want a guarantee buy a toaster at Macy's.

The future will be better tomorrow.

My fingers are too thick to text.

Jaytee weaving through the going-to-work morning action bumps into a man who is talking on his cell:

"Hey...no, not you, some guy is day dreaming and banged into me."

Jaytee stopped when he realized he almost knocked the guy over. "Sorry."

The man nodded and moved a far distance from Jaytee to an alcove of an unopened store. "Hold it, you're fading...this is better. No, I am not moving until you get what I am saying."

Jaytee realized where he was, the camera still hanging from his shoulder when he heard Nakhur, "You will know." Almost grateful to escape from Yanna's refusal, unaccustomed to vulnerable emotions, Jaytee decided to indulge, any activity that would divert his thoughts of Yanna, he raised the camera, saw that it presently arrowed to N, looked in the distance to the Man on the phone, on a wild impulse Jaytee moved the camera lever arrow to F for future, he pushed Record as the man carried on talking on the cell phone.

I am not into...that is stupid and dangerous in these times my baby. An open arrangement just leaves you and me, darling man, open to diseases I am loathe to mention and...yes, honey face, we can experiment but with each other. Of course I love you. Listen, I am late for work. Yes I'll pick up the wine, Later, my bitcherina.

He put the cell phone into his pocket and runs off, crossing the street at the exact moment of a car careening a turn against the light. The car hits the man who hurtles into the air, crashing on the pavement. Dead.

Jaytee takes the camera away from his eye, and looks at the man who is on his cell phone in the alcove of the unopened store. Jaytee is now in the zone as he moves the arrow to N and looks through the viewfinder, pushing Record as the Man talks.

"I am not into...that is stupid and dangerous in these times my baby. An open arrangement just leaves you and me, darling man, open to diseases I am loathe to......"

Jaytee pushes the lever arrow to B for past, Record:

In the priest's bedroom as 13-year old boy is crying quietly while the Priest undresses him and whispers while he caresses the shaking boy, "Love is patient, love is kind, love never gives up, never loses, faith...Corinthians 13:4-7, as the priest molests the tear stained whimpering boy.

Jaytee adjusts the lever arrow to N. Looks at the adult Man in the alcove talking on his cell. Record.

...yes, honey face, we can experiment but with each other. Of course I love you. Listen, I am late for work. Yes I'll pick up the wine, Later, my bitcherina.

He put the cell phone into his pocket and runs off, crossing the street...

Jaytee at effect of the past child abusive scene and his own instincts to do something other than deal with Yanna makes a wild dash and tackles/pushes the Man out of path of the careening car making a wild turn against the light. The car speeds away as a pedestrian observer yells at the departing car, "Pinche viea maldite cobarde." Jaytee helps the dazed Man up who is hyper-ventilating. "Oh my God, what was that. He almost killed me. You, thank you, you saved my life, oh my God, I was this close to being dead and oh God, Anthony will never forgive me if I died." Others came over to help as Jaytee, with camera, quietly walked away.

Jaytee entered his building, to his apartment door, again thinking, hoping, trying to ignore, unlocked the door and entered. No Yanna. Putting the camera down he sat on the bed, hearing his daddy, "There's something seldom about you, boy!"

He got up, undressed, went to the bathroom, pee'd, showered in water just a few degrees short of scolding, dried his body longer than necessary, left the bathroom, pulled the shades, put on a T-shirt and shorts, got into bed, trying to sleep despite hearing Yanna's accented voice saying I do not know what to do. Jaytee, buried his head in the pillow just as the sound of a key opening the lock of the door made him bolt upright.

The door swung open and carrying her suitcase and shopping bag of clothing Yanna stormed in, throwing everything on the floor breathlessly raging, "I am ready to work, I am good at anything, everything, what you call the land of opportunity is the land of social security number credit car driver license visa green card I am not a criminal I am strong woman who does not want something for nothing, job list in paper I apply and can do job good very good better but they want where I live address which I do not know have they want identification look at me I am identified as human being woman is that not enough!" She took a few needed breaths then looked up at Jaytee who was sitting on the edge of the bed with a smile that could light up a gloomy Sunday.

"Why are you smiling?" Yanna asked.

"Because this country boy is as happy as if he had good sense."

"Truth," Yanna provoked, "I can not stand lies."

"I don't bother lying, Yanna."

"Everybody lies," she insisted.

Jaytee shrugged, "If I don't be lying I don't have to remember about it."

"You are a strange man," she said.

"Thank you."

"I will stay if you want me to stay," she said more aggressively than she felt.

Jaytee moved from the bed, picked up her strewn clothes from the bag, he walked to the dresser and put some in the drawer, stopping to hear Yanna's disapproving sounds as he held up a dress he was folding to put in the drawer. Yanna came to him, took the dress out of his hands, opened the closet and found an empty hangar for the dress. Closing the closet door, her hands were shaking. She looked apologetically at Jaytee in his T-shirt and shorts, smiled wanly and held her hands to stop the shaking. Speaking in a quiet velvet tone, "Can you hold me, just hold me?"

Jaytee walking barefoot, reached out and held her as tears softly streamed down her cheeks onto his T-shirt. "I am soiling your shirt," she said between sniffles.

Jaytee pulled up the bottom of his shirt to wipe her tears. "I knew my shirt was missing something but I didn't know what 'til now."

"Thank you. You are a good man."

"And you are a good woman," Jaytee said.

"You do not know that yet," Yanna said, "But I am. A good woman."

They were quiet and for the first time comfortable with each other. She moved out of his arms, looked at Jaytee. "I have to ask once again more. Are you...do you need, want me to stay here, with you? No worries, doubts about this woman you do not really know?"

"Yes," he said. "Please do stay. With me."

Her eyes softened, listened as if some inner voice resounded, nodded her head as if agreeing with a decision, a first-time a small as it was smile, she talked in a whisper, as if she was about to reveal a secret. "You need sleep now yes?"

"Yes," he said.

"I me too. I have not slept good for too long to remember. Can we go to bed now?"

"Yes," he sad, "That would be good for this working man."

She looked at him with her head slightly tilted and a subtle sensual tone in her voice, "Do you have a shirt like that," she pointed at what Jaytee was wearing, "I can wear because I have nothing clean that would be...be what is the word...appropriate, yes, I want your appropriate shirt to bed."

Jaytee went to the dresser drawer, opened one and pulled out a T-shirt, which due to his size would work for most of Yanna's body. He turned to give it to her and saw Yanna dropping her clothing from her body, standing naked, as she held her hands out. "The shirt," she said gently, her eyes tender and welcoming.

Jaytee walked slowly to her nude body, put the T-shirt in her hands which Yanna held and with the shirt dangling from her fingers she embraced him mumbling, "I have not done this in a forever long time."

"If you want to wait, Yanna girl, this man ain't going anywhere."

"Now is a good time," she said tilting her face up to be kissed.

Six hours later, night, the shades still drawn, keeping the room in darkness. Yanna, in his T-shirt, rolled over in her sleep bumping into Jaytee. She opened her eyes in a moment of dread, cognized where and with whom...and just put her arm around his waist. Jaytee opened his eyes, caressed her hand on his body.

"Did I wake you?" she asked.

"Yes." He mumbled.

"I'm sorry."

"I'm not." He turned and took her into his arms as she snuggled into his shoulder.

"Can I tell you something very much terrible?" she whispered.

Jaytee holding her, "You can tell me anything."

"I like the way you feel inside of me. Very much. That is terrible to say, no?" she said coyly.

"So terrible, you may have to say it again, many times," Jaytee said.

"And you for me?" she asked.

"If I had a million dollars and a magic lamp granting me wishes that I could be anywhere with anyone, I would choose you, right here, right now."

"Good answer. I will stay."

"You better."

Yanna laughed for the first time in a very long time. "You will go to work soon?"

He nodded and started to move, "Soon, yes, I'll make us some breakfast."

"Will you let me do that?" Yanna asked.

Jaytee laughed and walked to the bathroom, "Let you? Shoot, that offer's as fine as frog's hair."

"Frog's hair?" she asked.

"Go for it, girl!" Jaytee laughed and went into the bathroom.

Yanna in his T-shirt and Jaytee dressed for work finishing a breakfast of toast, eggs, coffee, fresh squeezed orange juice. "You like? "she asked?

"I like the breakfast and I like Yanna even more."

"That is good."

Jaytee started to take the dishes to the sink when Yanna put her hand on his arm, "Let me."

"It just keeps getting better." Jaytee walked over and got his keys, wallet, and strapped the camera to his shoulder. "I'm on the way. You will be here when I come home, right?"

"If you want," she said with an easy smile.

"I want," and he started to go.

"Can I ask you something?"

"Anything," he said.

"The camera. From the first time I see you, always with the camera. Are you a photographer?"

"No, not really...just well...how can I put it...it's sort of a mystery, a secret I guess, someday I'll maybe tell you about it...but, yes I need to have the camera with me just in case..." and he trailed off.

"In case of what?" she asked.

"Sometimes, something...I just have to be able to use it at some particular times, I guess, that's the most I can tell you now."

"It sounds like a..." searching for the correct English words, "...a mission, is that the word, mission, are you a spy on a secret mission?"

He laughed, "A secret mission, okay. In a way maybe but not the way you're thinking, I'm not spying like in the movies..." he shrugged, "Maybe some time I'll be able to tell you but not just right now." He glanced at his watch. "As a matter of fact right now I have to go, won't be late." He walked to her, held her face in his hands, leaned down and kissed her, turned around and left.

Yanna threw up her hands and sighed loudly, with pleasure.

Jaytee driving the bus through the night city streets with the camera on the floor next to him. Many stops with passengers on and off. Jaytee is feeling good for obvious reasons, even enjoying hearing the lines from passengers:

He deserves no more than a tweet.

She has just the right amount of wrong if you get what I'm sayin'.

Je m'em fous.

Early morning as Jaytee comes out of the bus terminal, carrying the camera, gets on the bus heading home. He and driver nod to each other as bus moves through the city taking on passengers. Jaytee seated by the window holding his camera, thoughts of Yanna evoke a slight smile amid the snatches of conversation of riders to each other, some on their cells.

Who cares what happened to 20 years ago. Grow up!

Your idea of an agreeable person is someone who agrees with you.

I can't celebrate just because the calendar says so.

As the bus moved through a poorer section in town, stops accepting passengers, Jaytee looked out the window. He saw a homeless young Woman in front of a huge cardboard conglomeration which is her 'crash pad,' along with a shopping cart loaded with stained clothing and a stuff animal. Jaytee heard Nakhur, "You will know." He called to the driver, "Manny, I'll get off here."

"Hey, Jaytee, this turf ain't all that cool, man."

He got off the bus with his camera. "No sweat, Manny."

"If I don't see you tomorrow I'll put out an A-P-B on your ass." And drives the bus away.

Jaytee walked over to the young Woman who was eating what's left of a packaged 7-11 meal. She feels his presence and looks up at him. "Hey man, if you're seeking a cuddle-call you got the wrong girl." Jaytee says nothing but doesn't go. "This babesicle is only into A-B-C sex if that's what you're into."

Jaytee asked, "A B C?"

She cackled, "Anniversaries, Birthdays and Christmas so as you do not qualify and even if you got gigabucks on your person keep the motor going and wax with the wind, dude."

"I'm not interested in sex," he said.

"Sounds like deja-moo to me. You're at the wrong pit stop, mister. Don't be throwin' shade on me, dude!"

Jaytee heard Yanna's ...is that the word, mission, are you a spy on a secret mission...silently acknowledges just that as he asked the Woman, "How old are you?"

She sat up straight trying to be dignified in a setting that wasn't having any, "I am a legal adult which means old enough to know better and young enough to be stupid. You some kinda' freak of something 'cause you wasting your time bangin' on me as I got nothing' for ya.'"

Jaytee took out a ten dollar bill, "This is yours if I can take some pictures of you," as he held up the camera.

She looked at the ten, wanting it. "I don't be strippin' and I'm no pole dancer no matter whose pole but..." she grabbed the ten, "Take your pictures and for what some kinda' reality TV or something?" She mocked some bad attempts at a model's pose a few times, plastic smiles revealing a missing front tooth.

Jaytee adjusted the arrow to F or future. Record and looked through the viewfinder.

Woman sleeping in rolled up newspapers and ratty blanket, most of her body within the cardboard construction except for her feet sticking out.

Two guys grab her feet, pulling her screaming self out, ripping off her clothes, and go to rape her as she fiercely struggles.

Jaytee moved camera away, adjusts arrow to N and looked at the Woman who was posing as she strained, "Got your carrot or you want maybe another dynamite putting 'em away pose." She tired of her own act, "Fuck it, man, show's over."

Jaytee gave her another ten. "Just a few more shots."

She shrugged, "What the hell," taking the ten, "but I'm just gonna' be sittin' here contemplating my fucking future."

Jaytee adjusted the lever arrow to B for past, put the camera to his eye and pushed record.

In a living room as Young Woman's drunk step-father is beating her mother. She gets a nearby shotgun and screams, "Stop it, stop it!"

Drunken Step-father sees this and moves towards her, "You better know how to use that before I teach you a lesson like your messed up mama," whom he kicks as he goes towards the young Woman.

Mother grabs his ankle, "Don't hurt my baby."

He kicks her again, harder, and advances on Young Woman.

Young Woman holds shotgun and as Step-Father raising his fist, she fires. He falls back. Dead

Her mother groaning on the floor, "Call the cops. I shot him because he was beating on me. I did it. Say it. Mother shot him. Say it, girl!"

Young Woman crying, "Mother shot him."

JAYTEE MOVED THE CAMERA away from his face, adjusted the lever arrow to N. The Woman sat there bored. "You finished yet?"

Jaytee, moved by her past trauma asks, "Where do you want to go?"

She cackled, "I wanna' go crazy."

"That ride's already taken," Jaytee said.

The young tattered Woman looked around, "Somebody send you to mess with me. I can't be any more messed than this girl already is so give me some breathing room, dude."

"You can't keep sleep here. Where would you go if you had your druthers?" He asked.

"Are you for real or just a fig newton of my 'magination?"

"Where?" Jaytee pushed.

"Okay, weirdness deserves weirdness," she said, "How about Bakersfield, U.S.A.?"

Jaytee asked, "What's in Bakersfield?"

"My momma got out on probation. She needs some tending. Look at me, shoot, I can't pay for two hots and cot and I'm trippin' on...you got me teetering on the wrong end, dude!"

Jaytee came out of the Bus Terminal with a ticket, a bag of chips and some candies he got out of the machine, walked to the Woman who was sitting on the bench, gave her the ticket and chips, candies and another twenty. "This'll keep you until you get there." Bus leaves in twenty minutes.

She looked at him as if he was a ghost, waved it off and takes the ticket, candies and the twenty, "Why are you doing this, Mister?"

Jaytee walked her to the bus and said, "Don't think much of why I do things. Just do them."

"If this ain't legit magic my comedown will be a tsunami," she said.

"This here is your bus. Take care of Mama." Jaytee started walking away but she grabbed him in a feral hug. Stared into his eyes. Then ran into the bus.

Jaytee walked through the terminal and out into the morning city streets, snatches of conversation from passing pedestrians.

What's wrong with illusion, reality sucks!

Hey, I'm like a postage stamp, I stick until I get there.

A sound of a loud back-fire, similar to a gun shot, from a passing truck.

Jaytee flashed previous scenes with Woman shoots advancing drunk Step-Father.

Jaytee shook it off and continued gratefully through the many peopled streets.

Talking to you is like whispering to the deaf.

Ere un canal.

Jaytee walked by an appliance store with TV's playing a cop show with blasts a sound of gunfire. Jaytee flashed, Yanna screaming as she shoots oncoming Thug.

Jaytee stopped walking, sat down on a nearby stoop dealing with these recalls as the city action of traffic and people continue.

Now the shit's going to hit the fan.

Ahora va a estar mas cabron.

Hey man, they fatwa'd my butt.

Jaytee started walking again and heard sounds of someone singing and playing a guitar. He looked to the right and realized he was near the open air Market. He adjusted the strap on his camera and walked in and around many people, kiosks, easy action in the sun-lit day as he turned down one long opening to meet Nakhur who was carrying equipment for his stall. Jaytee said, "Can I give you some help, Mister?"

Nakhur nicely surprised, "Good to see you...Mister. Yes, you can carry some of this. Walk with me, Jaytee." Jaytee took some of the equipment as they walked.

Nakhur asked, "Your walk is heavy. Something distracting you?"

Jaytee smiled at his perception, walking. "Got me, yes. Okay, suppose just suppose after two there is some really deserving person who needs..."

"Two." Nakhur said sharply ending all possibilities.

They passed people talking.

Truth shall make you free, John 8:32.

Your truth put you in the slam.

Approaching the stall, Nakhur took the equipment from Jaytee and started arranging his kiosk.

Jaytee quietly shared, "I met a woman."

Nakhur arranged cameras on shelves. "Uhmm hmmm."

"She feels good," Jaytee said.

"She feels good?" Nakhur asked.

"What I mean is that when I'm with Yanna I feel good."

Nakhur dusting off some items, "How good?"

"Gooder than I ever felt. She hung the moon on my life."

Nakhur stopped, looked at him, "Yanna is your woman. Yes."

Jaytee entered his apartment, music playing from the radio, Yanna dancing and moving as she adjusted items, arranging the furniture, a new vase with flowers, and hanging an old parchment with Japanese lettering on the wall. She saw him, concerned about his response, said defensively, "If I am going to live here it must be some of me here."

Jaytee grinned, "I like it."

"True?"

"True."

"Good," Yanna said as she walked to Jaytee, taking his arms around her to dance.

"I don't know how to dance."

"I will teach you. Hold me tight."

"I can do that," as he holds and moves with her swaying body.

"Your body likes the music," she says in their belly to belly swaying.

"My body likes more than that." He kissed her and the casual kiss transformed into a passionate embrace.

In bed, after a fully satisfying erotic delicious sexual blending for both, Yanna was cuddled into his chest. "What means off the books?"

"I'm not sure."

"I got job. Waitress at Dave's Diner."

"Dave's, huh."

"Something wrong?"

"No, not at all," he said, "It's just two blocks away. I grab a bite there sometimes."

"Boss says he pay me off the books."

Jaytee got it, "Okay, since you don't have a social security number he won't report it. When do you start?"

"Tomorrow, when you finish work I start. I will pay half the rent."

"No way. But I will let you buy me dinner to celebrate."

"You have to loan me money until I get paid."

"I don't know," Jaytee played, "You may be too much of a risk. You'll have to put up some collateral"

Yanna punches him and they wrestle when he pins her underneath him. "What means collateral?"

They kissed playfully, "In case you don't pay, I get to keep something of yours."

"I have nothing," she protested.

His hand reached below her waist. "You have more than nothing."

"You dirty man."

"Guilty," as he caressed her sweet vagina.

Yanna purred, "I like dirty."

They made love with sounds, hands, tongues, in different positions, as 'dirty' as they both indulged in the visceral joy of sexual possibilities.

Hours later, the blinds drawn, Yanna sleeping, Jaytee walked quietly out of the bathroom dressed for work. He took his wallet, keys, picked up the camera, started to leave but stopped, considering thoughts, doubts, and then decided as he lifted the camera and adjusted the lever arrow to F for Future, looked through the viewfinder focusing on sleeping Yanna, pushed Record.

City streets close to midnight. Yanna as an OLD LADY carrying shopping bag, walking very slowly through the darkened streets. As old lady Yanna, in her slow old woman's gait crosses the street a wild car careens around the corner and she is directly in the path as car lights hit her frightened creased face, she lifts her arms as if to ward off the car.

The car swerves at the last moment, bypassing Old Lady Yanna who picks up her shopping bag and stuffs it with strewn items that fell out, walks as hurriedly as an old lady can walk to the other side of the street, entering a City Park, carrying the shopping bag walking, walking in the lonely shadowed park. Tired she sees, walks to a scarred bench and sits on it. Old Lady Yanna sitting on the bench. Alone.

Jaytee put down the camera at the sound of Yanna in bed moaning. He walked to the bed as she sat up in fear. Jaytee held her and whispered, "You just had a bad dream. Everything's okay, Jaytee's gonna change things for the better my Yanna, shhh, it's all okay, I got it covered."

Yanna realized it was a dream and buried her head in his shoulder, "Oh god I...it was...I am shooting gun and all I hear...gun shooting and cries from my baby never born. Oh God."

Jaytee held her, "I'm sorry, Yanna, but I promise...life will be better, I got yo' back."

Yanna muttered, "Some hurts never heal." She tried to shake it off physically and got out of bed. "I will make you breakfast."

"I got to go to work. I'll grab something on the way." He kissed her a light goodbye but she held him longer than usual, then released him, adjusting his hair. "Go, go." He stood there just looking at her. "What," she asked, "I look so terrible have not even brushed my teeth."

"You are beautiful," he said.

"I thought you never lie."

"I don't," Jaytee said.

"Good. Go to work," and kissed him passionately, shoved him playfully towards the door, and then stopped him. "No, I have to say something. You have time?"

He looked at her with great affection, "Shoot me a star, woman."

"Which means what?"

"I have nothing but time for my Yanna."

"Good because I must tell you...how can I say this...you change the toilet paper, you rub my back, you make me the morning coffee and stroke my head and hold me when I have terrible dream, you are like a man I have not known and that is why I must say to you, Jaytee, I am in loving with the best love man ever in my life."

Jaytee was surprised and moved by her declaration of love, although somewhat uncomfortable as he was unused to personal compliments.

Yanna sensed his discomfort, "You do not like me to say that Yanna loves Jaytee?"

He laughed. "I love hearing you say you love me. I'm just not all that you make me out to be."

"The word love is difficult for you to say?" she asked.

He realized that he never said that word. To anyone. Jaytee put his arms on her shoulders, leaned down so their face was on the same level, looked into her beautiful confused eyes, "Yanna, I never said the word love. To anybody. So get this girl, I, Jay Thomas Bergstrom, loves Yanna Ivanova and in my way we are as good as married which we will do on our days off in Vegas."

She broke out in a gleeful laugh, hugged him intensely, and this time pushed him out the door, "If you're late tell them that Jaytee's woman, Yanna Ivanova loved him into being late." As Jaytee, with camera, was going she called out to him, "Remember, I will be working at Dave's Diner when you are finished."

Jaytee did remember when his shift was over and instead of going straight home to an empty apartment, with camera dangling from the shoulder strap, decided to take a walk in the city park where a few joggers passed, some mothers pushed carriages, and some sitting on benches while their children played in the grass. Cutting across a ball field, walking through high grass and few trees he heard a child's voice, "Come on Fessie, it's all right, come on baby."

Climbing a tree was an 8-year-old girl with glasses, trying to retrieve her cat which seemed frozen on an extended limb too high up to reach from the ground. Jaytee watched the girl's fragile ascending journey up the tree, her cat not moving as she assured in her young tweedy voice, "You've been a bad girl but I'm going to get you, Fessie."

Jaytee observed, decided to indulge, lifted his camera, adjusted the lever arrow to F for Future and looked through the viewfinder as he pushed Record.

8-year-old Girl carefully climbing the tree, up and up until she arrives at the extended limb where Fessie is frozen, "Come on Fessie, come to Maya." Fessie the cat is frozen in fear as Maya inches forward on frail limb. "Well, okay...here I come." Maya slithers on thin limb extending far out. Limb is bending under her weight. "Please, Fessie, come to me, come on, I'll give you some goodies, promise." The cat does not move. Maya slithers further out on cracking limb

SNAP. Limb breaks.

Maya and Fessie come flying down.

SPLAT. Maya hitting the ground, glasses broke, blood oozing from her eyes, her shoulder and arm broken. Fessie the cat, who came out fine, goes to her, licking her face.

Maya cries out in severe pain, crying "Mommy...mommy..."

Jaytee pulled the camera away from his face and shouts loudly, "No!"

Maya in tree heard him and froze.

"The branch won't hold," Jaytee yelled.

Maya looked down and then at her cat and back to Jaytee, "Will you help me, Mister?"

Jaytee stopped, heard Nakhur, "Two times, that is all that is given. Two times." He hesitated.

Maya's entreating sweet petite voice, "Please, Mister, please?"

Jaytee took that cautionary breath and called to her, "Yes, I will help but first you have to come down."

"Promise to get Fessie down?"

Jaytee set the camera down and climbed up the tree, reaching his hand towards her. "Yes, now crawl back very slowly."

Maya inched backward, "It's scratching."

"You're doing fine, keep coming."

Maya freezes. "I'm scared."

Jaytee inching towards her but avoiding the fragile limb, "You're doing good, real good, now just keep creeping backwards, can you do that?"

She moved backwards very carefully, "Yes, I think so, yes." She gave it one final backward nudge and screamed as she was about to fall but Jaytee was near enough to catch her in his arms, sliding down the tree, setting her safe and sound on the grass. "There you go. You did good."

"You promised you would get Fessie down," she pleaded.

Jaytee nodded, climbed the tree to get to the level of the cat frozen in fear as Jaytee extended his arm and shook the brittle limb forcing the cat to fall onto lower limbs and landing safely on the ground when Maya scooped him up. "You have been so bad, Fessie, thanks Mister," and ran off with cat in her arms.

Jaytee, descending from the tree, but not his usual agile self. In fact it was so difficult it surprised him. He leaned down to pick up the camera, his back hurt a bit in his effort, he picked up the camera and on the back of the camera's large viewfinder he saw his image. A reflection of an OLD MAN.

Old Man Jaytee, carrying the camera, walked slowly through the park. Walking, walking with a slow steady old man's gait.

He returned to his neighborhood and walked to Dave's Diner to see Yanna who started work today. He walked in, looked for her, asked the woman at the register, "Where is Yanna?" he asked.

She responded, "I don't know any Yanna."

"She started work here today," Old Man Jaytee insisted.

"Old Timer," she said, everybody here's been working steady for years. No new waitress in a coon's age."

Jaytee nodded, turned and in the window saw the full bodied reflection of the old man he morphed into. He slowly walked out of the Diner.

In the open air Market shoppers, people watchers, kiosks filled with goods as Old Man Jaytee trudging slowly through the crowds carrying the camera to Nakhur's stand.

Nakhur was busy arranging cameras when Jaytee's old wrinkled liver spotted hands put down his camera on a shelf next to him. Nakhur turned and saw Old Man Jaytee and in sad recognition sighed. "You did Three." Jaytee nodded. Nakhur made a futile gesture as Old Man Jaytee turned and slowly ambled away hearing a customer at Nakhur's stand, "Is that camera for sale?" and Nakhur asking, "What do yo want. Out of life?

Old Man Jaytee continued walking through the throngs of mostly young people ignoring his old bearing.

Old Man Jaytee was tired of walking and sat by the window in the back of the bus which pulled into the Terminal. The Driver calling to the last passenger, "Last stop, old man."

Old Man Jaytee slowly rose and got off. He looked around and walked slowly toward a distant shadowed bench with an indistinct figure sitting on it. He tried to squint his eyes to see better but clarity did not come to his aged yellowing eyes, as he continued walking toward it.

Sitting on the bench was OLD LADY. Jaytee sat next to her, she reached into the shopping

bag, retrieved a thermos with hot chocolate, unscrewed the top, poured hot chocolate into a cup and gave it to Old Man Jaytee who took it and sipped, "Good," to which Old Lady Yanna simply said, "Yes, good."

A bus pulled up, door swish sound opening as the Driver called, "Getting on, folks?"

Old Woman Yanna looked at Old Man Jaytee, "Let's go home."

"Yes," Old man Jaytee said as they took each other's hands and slowly got on the bus.

As the bus drove off they were seated comfortably next to each other with a simple aura of belonging.

Don't miss out!

Visit the website below and you can sign up to receive emails whenever Rick Edelstein publishes a new book. There's no charge and no obligation.

https://books2read.com/r/B-A-JPFD-VCON

BOOKS 2 READ

Connecting independent readers to independent writers.

Did you love *Jaytee*? Then you should read *Manchester Arms*[1] by Rick Edelstein!

[2]

A recent college grad aspiring to be a writer— for material- gets a job as a Courtesy Assistant in an upscale residential hotel. The female and male residents challenge his moral and sexual parameters.

1. https://books2read.com/u/mV7k05

2. https://books2read.com/u/mV7k05

Also by Rick Edelstein

Scarlet Leaf Review Short-Story Anthology
Scarlet Leaf Review Short-Story Anthology Vol. I

Standalone
Jaytee

About the Author

Rick Edelstein was born and ill-bred on the streets of the Bronx. His initial writing was stage plays off-Broadway in NYC. When he moved to the golden marshmallow (Hollywood) he cut his teeth writing and directing multi-TV episodes of "Starsky & Hutch," "Charlie's Angels," "Chicago," "Alfred Hitchcock," et al. He also wrote screenplays, including one with Richard Pryor, "The M'Butu Affair" and a book for a London musical, "Fernando's Folly." His latest evolution has been prose with many published short stories and novellas, including, "Bodega," "Manchester Arms," "America Speaks," "Women Go on," "This is Only Dangerous," "Aggressive Ignorance," "Buy the Noise," and "The Morning After the Night." He writes every day as he is imbued with the Judeo-Christian ethic, "A man has to earn his day." Writing atones.

About the Publisher

It is based in Toronto and brings to public various books: poems, novels, short-stories, children's books, language study books and non-fiction. It publishes the literary review: Scarlet Leaf Review: www.scarletleafreview.com

Our mission is to help emerging authors and poets to make their works known to the public.

Contact   email   address: scarletleafpublishinghouse@gmail.com

www.ingramcontent.com/pod-product-compliance
Lightning Source LLC
Chambersburg PA
CBHW071202130626
46555CB00004B/1559